MANGA MATH MYSTERIES

(MATH)

THE LOST KEY

A Mystery with Whole Numbers

by Melinda Thielbar

illustrated by Tintin Pantoja

#1

GRAPHIC UNIVERSE™ · MINNEAPOLIS · NEW YORK

SAM
CARTER

AMY
TSANG

ADAM
BREGMAN

JOY
MEDINA

SIFU FAIZA

BRIAN NARATA

TOM JOHNSON

STACY LOWICKI

What is a **whole number**? Whole numbers are the **counting numbers** and also **zero**: 0, 1, 2, 3, 4, and so on.

We use whole numbers every day. We use them to count, add, subtract, multiply, and divide.

Story by Melinda Thielbar
Pencils and inks by Tintin Pantoja
Coloring by Hi-Fi Design
Lettering by Marshall Dillon

Graphic Universe™
A division of Lerner Publishing Group, Inc.
241 First Avenue North
Minneapolis, MN 55401 U.S.A.

Website address: www.lernerbooks.com

Library of Congress Cataloging-in-Publication Data

Thielbar, Melinda.
      The lost key : a mystery with whole numbers / story by Melinda Thielbar ; art by Tintin Pantoja.
          p.   cm. — (Manga math mysteries)
      Summary: When equipment is stolen from Sifu Faiza's Kung Fu School, where students learn compassion and responsibility as they train their minds and bodies, four friends use basic math skills to track down the culprits.
      ISBN: 978–0–7613–3853–6 (lib. bdg. : alk. paper)
      1. Graphic novels. [1. Graphic novels. 2. Mystery and detective stories. 3. Mathematics—Fiction. 4. Kung fu—Fiction. 5. Schools—Fiction.] I. Pantoja, Tintin, ill. II. Title.
PZ7.7.T48Lo 2010
741.5'973—dc22   2008053242

Manufactured in the United States of America
2 – DP – 2/26/10

7

KUNG FU SCHOOL

GOOD-BYE, SIFU!

GOOD-BYE, BOYS. I'LL SEE YOU NEXT TIME.

JOY, CAN I TALK WITH YOU FOR A MOMENT?

MY MOTHER IS VISITING THIS WEEKEND. BRIAN HAS TO GO TO WORK EARLY ON MONDAY. WOULD YOU AND YOUR MOM OPEN THE SCHOOL FOR ME ON MONDAY MORNING?

OF COURSE, SIFU.

COME ON, GUYS! WE WON'T STAY AT THE LAKE FOR VERY LONG!

I HAVE TO STUDY FOR MY MATH TEST ON WHOLE NUMBERS ON MONDAY.

BYE, ADAM!

COME ON, JOY! YOU CAN'T PLAY MARCO POLO WITH JUST TWO PEOPLE.

OK!

If kung fu makes you so smart, maybe you can figure out where we hid your stuff.

WHO COULD HAVE DONE THIS?

I HAVE TO CALL SIFU.

MOM, PLEASE POUR THE TEA WHILE I ANSWER THE PHONE.

RING RING

JOY, SLOW DOWN. I CAN'T UNDER-STAND YOU.

CLICK

DO YOU NEED TO GO HELP THEM?

SIFU MEANS "MOTHER" OR "FATHER" AS WELL AS "TEACHER." GOOD MOTHERS TEACH THEIR CHILDREN TO SOLVE THEIR OWN PROBLEMS WHEN THEY CAN.

DO THEY REALLY?

SIFU SAYS WE SHOULD TRY TO FIND THE EQUIPMENT.

SHE SAID TO START WITH WHAT WE KNOW.

Top shelf

Middle shelf
22 total slots.
11 slots have one T-shirt in each. The rest have one pair of shorts in each.

Bottom shelf
1 soccer ball.

Middle shelf
22 total slots.
11 slots have one T-shirt in each. The rest have one pair of shorts in each.
22 – 11 = 11 slots have shorts.

RING RING

HELLO?

I SEE.

WHAT DID SIFU SAY?

SHE SAID WE SHOULD TRY TO FIND THE EQUIPMENT. I KNOW YOU'RE SUPPOSED TO STUDY TODAY, BUT--

THAT'S OK. WHAT DO YOU NEED ME TO DO?

THE TEAM'S *SPONSOR* IS A BAKERY. THE BAKERY GIVES THEM MONEY FOR UNIFORMS AND SOCCER BALLS. THE BAKESHOP IS ACROSS THE STREET FROM COLONIAL HEIGHTS SCHOOL. THE TEAM PROBABLY PICKED UP THEIR NEW UNIFORMS THERE AND THREW THE OLD ONES AWAY.

SO IF THEY SWITCHED OUR STUFF WITH THE SOCCER STUFF, IT MIGHT BE IN THE DUMPSTER AT THE BAKERY.

COLONIAL HEIGHTS SCHOOL? THAT'S IN MY NEIGH-BORHOOD. THEY PICK UP THE TRASH ON FRIDAYS!

WE HAVE TO HURRY!

I'LL MEET YOU THERE!

WAIT! THERE'S NO WAY TO LOCK THE DOOR.

YOU GUYS GO AHEAD. I'LL WAIT FOR BRIAN.

?

WIDMAR AND SONS BAKERY

THAT MUST BE IT!

I'M GOING TO STAND UP. HOLD ON.

SIFU SAYS TO BE "LIKE A VINE." I'LL BE JUST LIKE A VINE-- I HAVE ROOTS, BUT I CAN BEND.

HAVE YOU SEEN A GARBAGE BAG WITH JUMP ROPES AND STUFF LIKE THAT?

I THINK SOMEONE THREW SOME THINGS AWAY BY MISTAKE.

SHAKE!

GOT IT!

Top shelf

Middle shelf
22 total slots.
11 slots have one T-shirt in each. The rest have one pair of shorts in each.
22 − 11 = 11 slots have shorts.

Bottom shelf
1 soccer ball.

HERE IT IS!

LET'S SEE WHAT'S IN THE BAG, AND JOY CAN TELL US WHERE IT GOES ON THE SHELF.

WE HAVE SOME JUMP ROPES.

THE JUMP ROPES GO ON THE TOP SHELF.

1, 2, 3, 4, 5, 6, 7, 8, 9, 10, 11. THERE ARE 11 SLOTS.

Top shelf
11 slots.

Middle shelf
22 total slots.

Bottom shelf
1 big space.

Top shelf
11 slots.
3 jump ropes for each slot.
11 × 3 = 33 jump ropes.

LET'S WORK ON THE SECOND SHELF WHILE ADAM COUNTS THE JUMP ROPES.

DON'T THE FOCUS MITTS GO ON THE SECOND SHELF?

WE PUT ONE FOCUS MITT IN EACH SLOT. THAT'S JUST MULTIPLYING BY 1, SO THERE SHOULD BE 22.

Middle Shelf
22 total slots.
1 focus mitt per slot.
22 × 1 = 22 focus mitts.

YOU'RE RIGHT. BUT YOU HAVE TO WRITE THAT DOWN TOO.

I'LL COUNT THE FOCUS MITTS.

I COUNT 22 FOCUS MITTS. WE HAVE ALL OF THEM!

JOY, DO YOU SEE THE BOXING GLOVES?

THE GLOVES ARE HERE.

BUT I DON'T SEE THE HEADGEAR ANYWHERE.

THAT'S RIGHT! WE ALWAYS STACK THE HEADGEAR ON THE BOTTOM SHELF. I USED TO MESS IT UP BECAUSE I THOUGHT HEADGEAR SHOULD GO ON THE TOP.

BUT WHERE COULD THE MISSING HEADGEAR BE?

1. Go 3 blocks South and tu

SALE 50¢

Go

I THINK WE KNOW WHERE THEY ARE.

OK. BRIAN IS HERE. I'LL HELP HIM LOCK UP AND MEET YOU AT THE FIELD.

OH, IT'S YOU!

36

9 total blocks divided into 3 equal parts.

Each part of the trip is 9 ÷ 3 = 3 blocks long.

41

Top shelf
11 slots.
3 jump ropes for each slot.
11 × 3 = 33 jump ropes.

Middle shelf
22 total slots.
1 focus mitt per slot.
22 × 1 = 22 total focus mitts.

Bottom shelf
1 big space.

42

Middle shelf
22 total slots.
1 focus mitt per slot.
22 × 1 = 22 total focus mitts.
2 mitts per pair.
22 ÷ 2 = 11 pairs of focus mitts.

Bottom shelf
1 big space.
1 helmet for each pair of focus mitts.
11 × 1 = 11 helmets.

The Author

Melinda Thielbar is a teacher who has written math courses for all ages, from kids to adults. In 2005 Melinda was awarded a VIGRE fellowship at North Carolina State University for PhD candidates "likely to make a strong contribution to education in mathematics." She lives in Raleigh, North Carolina, with her husband, author and video game programmer Richard Dansky, and their two cats.

The Artists

Tintin Pantoja was born in Manila in the Philippines. She received a degree in Illustration and Cartooning from the School of Visual Arts in New York City and was nominated for the Friends of Lulu "Best Newcomer" award. She was also a finalist in Tokyopop's Rising Stars of Manga 5. Her past books include a graphic novel version for kids of Shakespeare's play *Hamlet*.

Yuko Ota graduated from the Rochester Institute of Technology and lives in Maryland. She has worked as an animator and a lab assistant but is happiest drawing creatures and inventing worlds. She likes strong tea, the smell of new tires, and polydactyl cats (cats with extra toes!). She doesn't have any pets, but she has seven houseplants named Blue, Wolf, Charlene, Charlie, Roberto, Steven, and Doris.

Der-shing Helmer graduated with a degree in Biology from UC Berkeley, where she played with snakes and lizards all summer long. She is working toward becoming a biology teacher. When she is not tutoring kids, she likes to create art, especially comics. Her best friends are her two pet geckoes (Smeg and Jerry), her king snake (Clarice), and the chinchilla that lives next door.

AMY BY TINTIN

START READING FROM THE OTHER SIDE OF THE BOOK!

This page would be the first page of a manga from Japan. This is because written Japanese is read from the right side of the page to the left side of the page. English is read from left to right, so this is the last page of this Manga Math Mystery. If you read the end of the book first, you'll spoil the mystery! Turn the book over so you can start on the first page. Then find the clues to the mystery with Sam, Joy, Amy, and Adam!

MANGA MATH MYSTERIES #2

Somebody has stolen money from the soccer team. Everyone thinks Tom, the team's big bully, did it, but he says it wasn't him. Should Adam, Amy, Joy, and Sam believe him and help? They will have to figure out how much money was stolen—and also why! The kids work with dollars and cents to find . . .

The Hundred-Dollar Robber